ELIXIR OF LIFE

HOME OF EMOTIONS

BY

RUBICE ROSE

ISBN 978-93-5438-510-0
© RUBICE ROSE 2020
Published in India 2020 by Pencil

A brand of
One Point Six Technologies Pvt. Ltd.
123, Building J2, Shram Seva Premises,
Wadala Truck Terminal, Wadala (E)
Mumbai 400037, Maharashtra, INDIA
E connect@thepencilapp.com
W www.thepencilapp.com

DISCLAIMER: The opinions expressed in this book are those of the authors and do not purport to reflect the views of the Publisher.

AUTHOR BIOGRAPHY

Rubice Rose, A Passionate Teen Who Started Writting After Completing Her High School. A Medical Student Passed With Great Glorious Marks And Admitted In One Of The Prestigiou College Of Country, Does Not Have Any Literature Interest But We All Know We Never Choose Our Destiny, Destiny Chooses Us.

This Covid-19 Has Left A Great Impact On Everyone's Life . It Taught Everyone Difefrent Lessons. Some Have Lost Their Love One's And Some Lost Their Business But There In The Other Hand It Proved Good For Others Because Every Coin Has Two Side. Those Motivated Souls Who Have Passion To Do Something In This Pandemic Paved The Way, They Increse Their Interest To Passion, Some Grew Their Business ,Some Grew Their Brain Cells. Your Young Author Was Same, Through Her Interest She Built Passion And Here You Are Reading Her First Most Work.

Her Writting Is Unique Andd Simple From Others. Not A Complicated Method To Understand .Just Simple Rhyming With Simple Words But Deep Words. Maybe Like A Nursery Rhyme You Will Find It But Still Far Above From It.

 Being A Young Author ,New In Field Might Have Made Some Mistakes But Rest Assure Because Every Great Author Rise From Small. This Is Her Firist Small Ebook Containg Her Works She Did In This Wole Pandemic With True Emotions.Next Time

In Her Author Biography You Are Going To Read Her Achievements.

Be Safe ! Keep Supporting! Keep Smiling!

CONTENTS

The Little Chicken Inside Me

Brave Pain

Adernaline Rush

My Winterfluff

Relaxin Vibes

A Tasty Dopamine

INTRODUCTION

Home Of Emotions

Thank You For Choosing This Book To Know Your Emotions . Every One Have Diffrent Emotions And Different Reasons Behind Them But Same Series Of Thoughts. In This Book You Will Get To Know "Do We Actually Think Same Or Is It Me Who Feel Like This Is Me?" .

Elixir Of Life, To Be Scientific This Stands For A Medicine Which Is Used To Become Immortal . The First Question Arises, Why It Is Used Here? First Of All It's Not Our Breath Who Make Us Immortal , Our Thoughts, Our Passion,Our Works,Our Deeds Amd Lastly Our Emotions Make Us Immortal. Immmortal Means "Being Alive For Forever" . The Above Mentioned Things Make It Possible For Us To Be An Immortal.

Emotions Is Whole New Thing You Have Heard Included In Being Immortal. Our Every Emotions Is Passed From One To One. One's Passionate Emotions Like Mahatma Gandhi's Passion To Free India Is Passed To Us Till Now. Abraham Licoln Desires Are Still Passed To Us And Many More.

This Book Is Mainly A Peotry Book Which Consist Of Sort Of Poems Representing Difeerent Emotion. Emotions Doesn't Come From Inside Always, They Are Attached To Someone Speacial To Us Too And Mainly 'They' Are The Reason Behind Our Emotions .From Small Poems With Difrrent Wrtting Stlyes The Author Tried Best To Express In One Go.

Humans Are Liek A Pot Filled With Emotions And A Filled Pot Is Always Tresured So We Should Always Keep Smiling ,Feeling Emotions. It's Written Nowhere That If You Are Man You Can't Cry .It's Written No Where That Your Maturity Is Defined By Seriousness. Humans Are Made With Emotions ,They Are Grown Up With Emotions Then What's Wrong With Living With Emotions. Expresssing Emotions Is Most Important Because Life Is No Fun Without Them. So Express Yourself More , Smile More,Cry More,Shout More! Everything Is Okay Untill An Unless You Are Okay. Hiding And Controlling Your Emotions Won't Help You,It Will Bury Your Heeart In Deep Pit And Weigh You Down. I Hope You Understand What Author Wants To Convey You.

This Book Starts With The Emotions Which Are Brought By Our Love One's That Is Our Family. From Mother To Father And To Sibling's Role Played In One's Life. Thousands Of Words Are Not Enough To Describe Their Importancee In One's Lief But Here Author Shared Just Litlle Deep Words And A Short Incident For Her Sibling.

The Second Part Of Book Consist Of Book Consist A Story Of A Black Girl . A Pure Soul But Still Get Attacked By The Harsh And Shitty Rule Of Society. From Her Child Hood To Young Age Every Emotions She Felt Are Described Beautifully By Author. A Poem About Her Insecurity . A Poem About The Devilish Side Of Thoughts And Emotions Are Also Described Although It Has Nothing To Do With The Girl But She's Also Subjected In That Expression. Author Has No Intensions To Hurt Someone's Feeling And If She Did Then A Heartfelt Sorry From Her Side.

The Third Part Is All About The Author's Inspiration . Who Have Inspired Her And Who Have Make Her Keep Moving On. A Emotion Of Struggle Is Expressed By Author Via A Poem About Artist. They Might Be Known Or Unknown To You But For The Sake Of Humanity No Judgments And No Hatered Because Your Hate Might Be Someone's Life Line And They Sure Haven't Done Something For You But They Are Someone's Comfort In Tough Time And Warmth In Cold Days. I Hope You Respect Author's Feelings.

Everyone Have Inspiring Souls. What Are Yours ?

 The Last Part Consist Of Emotions Truely Felt By Author. From Sadness To Happiness. From Low Point To High. Everything Is Pictured Beautifully By Her Words.

Happy Reading! Happy New Year! Always Express Emotions!

PREFACE

Hello my precious readers, thank you for choosing this short poetry book. "The Elixir of Life~Home of Emotions". TO be honest I never thought I would be writting a book and that too a poetry book. it's suprising as well as exciting. Neither I have qualified any poetry compitition nor any academics . Then it might strikes to your mind that how came i wrote this book ? well I started writting during the pandemic , my first poem "The Lustfull youth". I Shared my poem to my friends and relative, I made blogger account and published there. I got a good review and some of my relatives even called me next instant, I send them my poem ,to confirm if it was really me. they encouraged me and said to write more and more and never drop this practice.

I then made accounts on social media to make my work more appraochable and it did. I got amazing reviews and feedback that all of my readers suggested to publish my work. At first I was insecure like I was new in this field and on top of that my poems weren't usual long and different ,they were simple and rhyming but still one of my friend insisted.

After a long thinking i arrived at conclusion that I should publish my poems and as I have only limited poems so I decided to make a short one. I am emotional type person so I thought my first book should be on something like that and here it came my first ever poetry book describing different emotions in different waYs but similiar to your.

I could have made a long one too but I wanted to publish this book on particular date due to some one special's birthday so I kept it short.

It's not a complex book,simple poetry book you might complete in short time but feel the words, the emotions I wanted to convey to you. read out a poem which you feel that's what your emotion is at that particular time. trust me it will hit hard.

The book's motive, well there are some poems which are mainly for taunting the evil thoughts and acts in our society.No doubt we have advanced in many sector but still there are many fields in which we are stick to our past low thinking, which shouldn't be like this. I have mentioned some of them ,hope you get the message and change your attitude . Our actions might hurt those precious souls who have done nothing wrong.our mere smile won't hurt but our expression acts more than any physical action.we should be thankful for every single thing we got . a thanking attitude is also I want to induce in you because nothing last forever. Guilt is feeling which is worst and no one wants to feel it. So a thanking nature should be our main character ,that's what make us human.

PART A

Emotions Of Home

1. Infinite Love

2. The Strongest Feather

3. Crazy Pill

INFINITE LOVE

She brace the pain of menstruation,
To become one of the best creation.

Abandon her family to cohere another,
Never learnt but masters in couther.

Fake her happiness for the sake of one's ,
Put other's first whether she come after tonnes.

Hear their taunt without complaining,
Just because she got house for maintaining?

She asked for love only to get ignored
could give her all happiness, that she deserved!

Raising us from zygote to man,
She lost her origin from where she began.

Isn't it ironical how she suffers in our problems?

Just to give us fragrance, she lost her blossoms.

I salute from heart to her divinity,

That's her love which I call 'INFINITY '.

THE STRONGEST FEATHER

Borned in a patriachal family,
Alot cried but he rejoyced happily!

Like a campfire in winter days
He comforted me in every ways.

My knight in shining armor,
True reason behind my glamour.

Spoiled for them but innocent for him,
Never for a sec. he let me dim.

Sweet or sour ,every candy was on his list,
Even in saddest story he brought the twist .

All stressed and wornout,
Just to make his lil seeds sprouts.

Never let anyone to see his tears,

Branded for us but cheap he wears.

Love for mom,strength to brother,
Everything to me so didn't write another.

CRAZY PILL

A normal morning for sweeping the house,

Where my brother was just irritating me like a mouse...

"Yah ! You brat!! " I shout turning back,
He just laughed, " oh I think you wanna smack? "

" Get lost!! Before I lose my temper! "
"But sis! You have to tolerate my pamper! "

My eyes were red like vampire,
After a while he left for entire..

I shut the door for the peace,
There was a knock again " Oh! He's just a tease! "

" I swear I'm gonna kill you " Jack,
"oh Sweety! Calm down! " my mom shouted back!!

" you lil brat! Jerk! Just wait"

Holding my broom high I opened the gate

"I Swear i love from my brain to heart my sis " he said.

I let him in but "i don't have brain dumbhead" he replied making me mad.

PART B

A SEXUAL PREJUDICE

Craving for a doll was really much,

A black girl like me only wanted their delicate touch...

"you're a girl Sweety! Know your limits!

" A black like you is just to omitt!!!

Their words stabbed me like a dagger,

But my soul was rigid still my mind was stagger!!

My white brothers were always their priority

As if I was intruder in their territory!??

I felt my voice refused to unfold,

Because my existence truth was just untold....

God gives two eyes for an equal vision,

One mouth to prevent the division..

Still my thought are lingering outside,

" will I ever be free? " a heavy pain was still inside

A poor heart of mine wasn't that strong,

Just asking the world "what I did wrong? "

A LUSTFUL YOUTH

Sitting on the roof alone,

Wonder where do I come from..

A small child with sincere smile,

To a selfish person whom I want to forget for a while...

"Ah!! That's what I want! ",

Which now become a lusty demand and they Grant???

With a cheerfull hope on a face,

Now I try to keep up with the pace..

A delicate heart like a feather,

Undergo with different thunderstroam and weather...

Mirror reflecting the sparkling of eyes,

Lost the zeal in the journey of becoming wise...

"I'm sorry! " to hold the relation,
To "Do what you want!! " and went for vacation!??

A kid having words of love,
Now masters in manipulating the dove?

A loveable and humble personality,
Now greedy for formalities????

Sitting on the roof I thought?!,
Wonder where that child got lost???

A TRAIC TRANSITION

Her smile,

Her tears,
Her every single fear,

Neither one was right!!!

Her sincerity,
Her laugh,
Her inner baff,

Neither one was light!!!

Her moves,
Her eyes,
Her self disguise,

Neither one was bright!!!!

Her vibes,

Her little walk,

Her childish talk,

Neither one was Alright!!!

Her anger,

Her dejection,

her visual perception ,

Neither one was slight!!!

Her anxiety,

Her intimacy,

Her pure innocency,

Neither one was alike!!!!

MY JUDGMENTS

"Have you seen yourself in mirror?" there i am!
Too ugly, even no effect of beauty cam!!

"Too fat! eat a bit less pig!" they taunts,
Even after loosing weight their words still haunts!

"bit more fair skin without ache or plastic surgery will do" they
laughed,
"Am I that bad? should I stay at home,locked?"

It's been years those things happened and I changed,
Still can't love myself and appreaciate ! THAT'S how much I AM
tamed!

My speaking to walking ,nothing to be praised!
"then why the hell I'm here! why they raised?"

Academics weren't my field and sports are too far to think.
"should I END it here ?" I thought but i heard a click?

" Your worth is your heart, body is just piece of cotton~"

"Once get wet,settled down hence remain forgotton!"

"Words do change life and they changed mine!"

I AM WHO I AM ! so let's celebrate with wine!

DEVIL DISGUISE AS DISGUST

Smiling & laughing after painting his face with cake,
being irritated by hungry voice of children which seemed fake.

"Let's give some to them" one of said to interrupt,
"ignore them!they just want attention~let's go" we said being
corrupt.

No guilt no shame after leaving hungry souls behind,
"how does it feels being helpless!" he said again to remind.

"look dude,they can work and earn by themselves! pathetic
poor~"
"If onlt you have heart to except their proposals for real!"

Too itchy, too smelly ! we are allergic to them.
In reality, only to left the ego we have in our hem.

"Look those third gender! auk! it's grosss~"
"you also have one in your family from where you arose"

"They are mistake in science and shame on human!"

SO Does your disgust make you real one?

PART C

Inspiration

A GOD GIFTED HEALER

Being in the lap of nature ,
Most amazing thing for a creature .

The cold breeze brushing off the hair ,
All the negativity get vanished leaving behind care.

Tall and strong trees standing like armor,
Making our mind more quieter and calmer .

Chirping of the birds is really melodious,
To our ear it's healthy and commodious .

The fallen leaves are attractive piece of art ,
The joy of adventure lies in riding a cart .

Weeds didn't go unnoticed by me,
Making my life worth talking over a tea .

let's talk about a Landscape ,

It brings our soul in it's best shape.

Every single thing is inspiring here,

Still our gratitude towards nature is mere !

A BULLETPROOF POEM

Just   a silhouette, when we first step in,

Never knew we'll own this much win...

From starving and fighting together,

Now they all ask " would you like rather?"

Like a rookies we came in this industry,

Rocked the whole world and made them thirsty...

Followers were sure 500 once,

It's our determination which turned them into tonnes..

Singing and composing in one room,

I never thought this much we can bloom...

Haters were more than lovers,

Now we're the only one on the covers,,

A fading thought of leaving was in our mind,

But we made it together through all this kind..

"It's not your game babies" we heard,

Why? " this game is own by us! " we roared..

"just once" thought to shine,

God planned more so that's fine...

Once not twice not thrice we were mess,

But our army made us The B. T. S.

THE IMMORTAL TEACHER

My morning excitement reaches to peak!

Reason to boost me up through early morning scenery! call me

freak?

Clouds dispersed having bright incident light,

Made me dance in happiness forgetting every fight!

I listened to crazy talks of birds before rise,

Making plan to fly a marathon &win SUN as prize.

After anticipation the sun rises above the horizon

Vanishing every darkness and sadness with his crimson.

Saluting him for his bravery i said with confidence.

"LET ME BRIGHTEN UP THIS WORLD WITH

HAPPINESS TO CHANGE THE PREFERENCE"

Darkness will engulf again but you gonna rise again,

Every struggle add stairs towards your aim not letting it go in

vain !

Burning alone you still stand high in the sky,

Teaching me "fail &gain" because my plan worth try.

Even if clouds shadow your rays ,

You beautify the sky in your own unique ways.

Once again that fog dimmed your brightness,

We got your lesson "rise and shine again" my highness.

PART D

My "Gamjeong"

1. Water Sheds

2.Rollercoster Ride

3. The Little Chicken Inside Me

4.Brave Pain

5. Adernaline Rush

6.My Winter Fluff

7. Relaxin' Vibes

8.A Tasty Dopamine

WATER SHEDS

Wonder How Child Gets In Clothes They Wear ?
It's Even Hard To Control My Tears.

Eyes Filled But Still Can't Pour Down,
I Swear I Never Wished For Crown!

Don't Need Disease To Suffocate Me,
My Tears Are Enough To Spill The Tea.

Isn't It Amazing To Laugh In Pain?
And Next Moment It Can Make You Insane!

Hearing Quarelles And Judgments Are Routine,
It's Too Much For My Heart!I Am Still A Teen!

Holding Back My Tears I Spoke To Them!
Does My Decision Matter? Anyways They Gonna Condemn!

Wasn't New To Be A Victim,

My Happiness Lights Were Already Dim!

At Last I Bid A Adieu ,
Today's Night Is To Pour My Heartue!

My Life Isn't That Dry!
It's Just, Sometimes It's Okay To Cry.

ROLLER COSTER RIDE

Once I'm feeling so high!

Then I feel like "bye? "

"Heyo! My buddy?" I exclaim!!
"don't bother me! " that's me too for blame!

"I 'm trash " ,feeling so down!
And then "I am talented!! " like I own the crown!

"they don't love me anymore! "
"Oh I don't care they're just bore!! "

" it's amazing! " I love citylight,
"It's dull",city contains only plight!

I'm introvert!, I love loneliness!
Let's go outside to relieve some stress!!

Reading books and stuffs aren't my type!?

Yoo!! Books are cool way to wipe!!

"Am I good? Am I perfect? "

"Bro! I still left a great impact!! "

THE LITTLE CHICKEN INSIDE ME

The lights on the road were sparkling like stars,

Still the darkness was corroding me like a cigar..

Although people accompanied me everywhere,
A felling of loneliness was really bizarre..

Those smiles melt my heart deep to the core,
Want to smile like them freely, as mine
was fake which I wore..

Many were holding up me like a pillar,
But, for me, those all appeared like a glimmer...

My tears were assuredly torning them apart,
"it's fine! It's ok, not to be smart! "

Words were messed up in my mind,
None strikes my question for solution to find..

"God will appreciate when the right moment comes"
My accuracy wasn't enough, so I never listened to mums!

They told a little more won't hurt,
"HOW?, when my eyes were tired from blart...

"Our hopes are high on you! Never give up! "
"that's my biggest fear ",I never wanted to be a pup...

BRAVE PAIN

Once again i squirmed around my bed,

"I swear ! it's not good being girl!" I begged .

Clutching my stomach which is paining like hell ,

I felt like creature FROM whom we take out the pearl.

Nausea and diarrhoea " is anything left more?"

thousands of emotions shaking me from my core .

A crapm striked and sob left my lips,

Just wanna this pain fade away ,"have any tips?"

Being honest , i felt like shit!

Everyone left me alone but not for grabbing the kit!

Telling my situation to them is 'embarrasing?'

i cried and shouted ! waited for happening, nothing?

"Let her be! She's in her monthly !" they exclaimed,

I just wanted them beside me ! Is this what i gained?

Blood flowing out from my body,
Are you sure it's easy being 'lady'?

To be a mother , we gotta go through it!
being digusting and rude ? Jut stop behaving like shit!

many tears are left unnamed ,

"I Am Strong To Bear This Alone! Why To Be Ashamed ?"

ADERNALINE RUSH

Fast beating heart ,raising chest with heavy breaths,
"I swear I am too young to have a facetime with death"

Legs were shaking! from running or fear or both?
"hey~ there's place to hide! In that tree's growth !"

Goosebumps over body and sweat over forehead
Every emotions is overwhelming just tears left to shed !

"Hey there's peace in death I heard~" My friend cheered!
"You go first ,I am still unmarried " I back fired.

My pupil enlarged & breath hitched over those faint sound of
crushing leaves !

My heart dropped on thought that I never gave shits to rituals
and believes .

"Calm down heart , I think I once thanked GOD!"

Begging to spritiuals above "Just save me MY LORD!"

"Let's stop breathing? it might help?"
that thing came nearer and nearer making me yelp!

"Hold on ~ life isn't that short for you"
That moved on and heavy sigh left our mouth one after two!

MY WINTERFLUFF

Just a wish to hug all day long &call you mine,

the feel when I look into your eyes is stronger than any wine.

Could spend dollars to see your smile !

How does it feels if you worry about me for a while?

At first i smiled when i would see you,

Now my happiness doesn't know who isn't you

From dreaming to prayers you have become more than a habbit!

Just wanna adore you like lil child do to a rabbit

Well wishes for you and stress for me,

If there's a way to take your pain ,i wanna steal that key!

Call me obsessed or blind in love ?

You name make me glow without any 'dove'.

My prayer starts from you and ends at us!

I would be honored to become even a imposter for you in

'among us'

If by faith we get together !

Not any fancy date but a lovely walk in any weather.

RELAXIN VIBES

Breathes it's been awhile I felt like me,
Sitting alone and eyeing the city view makes me free.

My beating heart and city rush boh seems quite,
I devoured the taste of chocolate after taking a bite.

Closing my eyes , I let the cold breeze engulf me in it's arms,
Got lost in the sweet melody of nature and astonishing charms.

I felt amuzed how every inch of my body responded,
Me and nature seemed same as if we were bonded.

My eyes sparkled and lips twitched to smile.
I sensed myself walking alone many miles.

Goosebumps took over my body,
A faint voice in my heart said "are you ready?"

I stand up with more confidence and energy,

This is what THE result of intractive synergy!

A TASTY DOPAMINE

Dancing and squirming around my room,
I felt like my stupid friend finally found a groom!

Everyone appears singing a merry song~
I am smiling like maniac "what's wrong?"

Just felt the urge to praise every lil thing?
Even the rat who bother's my sleep seems cute ~ "eww cringe"

"If you say sorry i might forgive you?" i texed my ex!
"wow! yo seems in good mood ~ mind paying my tax?"

"Oh my brother how comes you are too sweet~"
"y-you sure y-you aren't on drugs? j-just quit!"

"Don't you think I should apply for Miss world?"
I praised myself only to get command from mom to buy curd!

"'OH how come streets are too beautiful?"

"it's same lady, just you are too cheerful"

"Chocolates and cakes and yeah the curd for sure please!"
I asked being gullible forgetting that he just sneezed!"

"What happened you seems happy? had shot?"
" No --w-wait! MY ASIGMENTS OH GOD!!"

List Of Contributors

A Heartful Thank You To My Mom And Dad ***Mr. And Mrs. Manjhu*** .Who Supported Me And Encouraged Me To Write My Emotions And Amke It Publish . Thanks To My Wach And Every Readers Who Motivated Me To This Pointthat I Am Here Writting This To You.

Speacial Thanks Goes To My Freind ***Aditri S.*** Who Helped Me All Way Long And Was There For Me At Every Point ,Whenever I Needed Help . Thank You So Much Precious.

Also The Pencil Team Who Made My Dream Comes True . Thanks A Lot

I Love You All From The Deepest Core Of My Heart!